SOME SNOW IS...

ELLEN YEOMANS

ANDREA OFFERMANN

putnam

G. P. PUTNAM'S SONS

Some books are sibling books. For Brad, Jeff, and Laura. They know snow. —E.Y.

For Elsa, Michel, and Nissi. —A.O.

G. P. PUTNAM'S SONS
an imprint of Penguin Random House LLC, New York

G. P. Putnam's Sons is a registered trademark of Penguin Random House LLC.

Visit us online at penguinrandomhouse.com

Library of Congress Cataloging-in-Publication Data
Names: Yeomans, Ellen, 1962– author. | Offermann, Andrea, illustrator.
Title: Some snow is . . . / Ellen Yeomans; illustrated by Andrea Offermann.
Description: New York, NY: G. P. Putnam's Sons, [2019]
Summary: Illustrations and easy-to-read text celebrate all of the different kinds of snow,
from the snow that melts as soon as it hits the ground to packable "Snowman Snow."
Identifiers: LCCN 2018028168 | ISBN 9780399547546 (hardcover)
Subjects: | CYAC: Stories in rhyme. | Snow—Fiction. | Winter—Fiction.
Classification: LCC PZ8.3.Y463 Som 2019 | DDC [E]—dc23
LC record available at https://lccn.loc.gov/2018028168

Manufactured in China by RR Donnelley Asia Printing Solutions Ltd.
ISBN 9780399547546
10 9 8 7 6 5 4 3 2 1

Design by Dave Kopka.
Text set in Laurentian.
The art was done with pen, ink, and watercolor with digital touches.

Some snow is First Snow.
We've waited for so long snow.
Is it really *snow* snow,
    or only heavy rain?

It's hit the ground and melt snow.
We know it's only time snow.
We'll watch and wait it out snow
    until it can remain.

Some snow is Sleet Snow.
Fast and icy wet snow.
Slushy, mushy fake snow
not good for anything.

Some snow is Fluff Snow.
Wind blows and it goes snow.
But soon will come the True Snow
we'll use for everything.

Some snow is Angel Snow.
Finally covers all snow.
Light and slightly deep snow—
    drop down and make some wings.

Arms fly up and down snow.

Legs sweep along the ground snow.

Move and flop again snow;

a flock of angels sings.

Some snow is Snowball Snow.
Stick it, pound it, play hard snow.
Gather more for forts snow,
    call all your friends, and then—

Break up into teams snow.

Make piles before you throw snow.

Whizzing back and forth snow,

    then scoop and pack again.

The worst snow is Driveway Snow.
Papa growls and grumbles snow.

Doesn't he remember snow
from when he was a kid?

We will help him shovel snow.
Why is this such heavy snow?
Almost never-ending snow...

but see what we just did.

Some snow is Tracking Snow.
Look for signs of critters snow.
Could be something big snow,
   or something rather small.

Some snow is Yellow Snow.
Stay away from *that* snow!
You really need to know snow,
'cause that was one close call.

Some snow is Sledding Snow.
Nothing slows me down snow.
Hop on board, push off snow,
face freezing as you race.

It's take your breath away snow.
Fly on down the slope snow.
Tumble off the sled snow,
    trudge up a slower pace.

The best snow is Snow Day Snow.
Can't go out in that snow.
Too much coming down snow,
a world of swirling white.

We'll play games and draw snow.
Read our books and dream snow.
Watch the streetlights glow snow,
a winter-quiet night.

Some snow is Snowman Snow.
Roll it, pack it, stack it snow.

Build him right out front snow:
two sticks, a scarf, a heart—

Then smooth and pat it down snow.

Hat and carrot nose snow.

Enjoy him while he lasts snow. . .

until he falls apa r t.

Soon it will be Spring Snow.
Grass and mud and rain snow.
Time to go away snow;
     no more lingering.

Soon, soon, all gone snow.
We've waited for so long snow.
Please, please, no more snow . . .

our bikes are whispering.